When Bad Snakes
Attack Good Children

Don't miss the other spine-tingling
Secrets of Dripping Fang adventures!

SECRETS OF

DRIPPING FANG

BOOK EIGHT

When Bad Snakes
Attack Good Children

DAN GREENBURG

Illustrations by SCOTT M. FISCHER

HARCOURT, INC.

Orlando   Austin   New York   San Diego   Toronto   London

*I want to thank my editor, Allyn Johnston, for her macabre yet soulful
sense of humor, for her eagerness to explore ideas beyond the bounds of taste,
for understanding an author's poignant thirst for praise, and for helping
me say exactly what I'm trying to say, except more gooder.
I also want to thank Scott M. Fischer,
an artist with dizzying technical abilities and a demented genius
at combining terror and humor in the same illustration.*
—D. G.

Text copyright © 2007 by Dan Greenburg
Illustrations copyright © 2007 by Scott M. Fischer

www.HarcourtBooks.com

Library of Congress Cataloging-in-Publication Data
Greenburg, Dan.
Secrets of Dripping Fang. Book eight, When bad snakes attack good
children/Dan Greenburg; illustrations by Scott M. Fischer.
p. cm.
Summary: Followed by an assassin and her poisonous snakes,
ten-year-old twins Wally and Cheyenne Shluffmuffin try to get
from their Ohio home to the FBI training facility in Quantico,
Virginia, to get help in freeing human hostages from the onts.
[1. Assassins—Fiction. 2. Poisonous snakes—Fiction. 3. Orphans—
Fiction. 4. Twins—Fiction. 5. Brothers and sisters—Fiction.
6. Cincinnati (Ohio)—Fiction.] I. Fischer, Scott M., ill. II. Title.
III. Title: When bad snakes attack good children.
PZ7.G8278Sei 2007
[Fic]—dc22 2006035430
ISBN 978-0-15-206056-5

Text set in Meridien
Designed by Linda Lockowitz

First edition
A C E G H F D B

Printed in the United States of America

For Judith and Zack
with spooky love

—D. G.

Contents

When Bad Snakes
Attack Good Children

CHAPTER 1

The Man Who Knew Too Much—or, Possibly, Too Little

The face of the woman behind the reception desk at FBI headquarters in downtown Cincinnati was oddly familiar and a bit unsettling. Something about her skin didn't look quite right. It looked like the skin of a dead person. It looked like you could peel her face right off her skull.

"Yes, may I help you?" asked the woman, but there wasn't much help in the voice.

"We're Wally and Cheyenne Shluffmuffin," said Wally. "We're here to see Special Agent Cromwell."

"And you have an appointment?" said the woman.

"Well, no, but we've been here before," said Wally. The Shluffmuffin twins were ten years old, had red hair and freckles and a tendency to attract creatures with sinister intentions, most of whom were not even human.

"And what was this in reference to?" said the woman.

"Well, we gave him some pictures," said Cheyenne.

"Pictures . . . ?"

"Of the six buses that disappeared in downtown Cincinnati," said Cheyenne. "And pictures of the people who were on the buses when they disappeared. Agent Cromwell said he was going to show them to people in his department and then get back to us, but we haven't heard from him in over two weeks."

"And these pictures were taken where?" said the woman.

"It doesn't matter," said Wally, deciding against saying they were taken in the cave of the

Ont Queen, ruler of all giant ants in the state of Ohio. "Can we just please see Agent Cromwell?"

"No."

"Excuse me?" said Wally.

"Special Agent Cromwell no longer works here," said the woman.

"No? What happened to him?" said Cheyenne.

"He's dead."

"Dead?" said Cheyenne. "But we just saw him two weeks ago. He seemed fine."

"Yes, two weeks ago he *was* fine," said the woman. "But now he's dead. It was very sudden. Sudden and tragic. We were all quite stunned."

"What did he die of?" Wally asked.

"Heart attack," said the woman, suddenly losing interest in the discussion and turning back to papers on her desk. "Is there anything else? I'm afraid we're quite busy here today."

"Who's taking over for Agent Cromwell?" Cheyenne asked.

"Nobody."

"Well then, can we at least get our pictures back?" Cheyenne asked.

"And what pictures would those be?" said the woman, studying her papers.

"We just told you," said Wally. "Pictures of the six buses that disappeared downtown?"

The woman reached into a drawer, pulled out some printed forms, and held them out to the twins without looking up.

"Fill these forms out in triplicate," she said, "stating what property you are claiming and the circumstances under which you are claiming it, attaching a notarized statement of value and a proof of loss form, and then we will process your claim. When the process is complete, somebody will be in touch with you."

"And when do you think that might happen?" asked Cheyenne, taking the forms.

"Twelve to fourteen weeks," said the woman. "This is our busy season."

"Never mind," said Cheyenne. She gave back the forms.

———

As soon as they got into the elevator and pushed the down button and the doors slid closed, Wally announced: "Cromwell was murdered."

"Are you sure?" Cheyenne asked.

"I'm positive."

"But why?" Cheyenne asked.

"He knew too much."

"How do you know that?" Cheyenne asked.

"I just know," said Wally. "He either knew too much or he knew too little. He didn't know just enough. If he had known just enough, he'd be alive today."

"How much is just enough?" said Cheyenne.

"That is something we will never know," said Wally.

"You think it was because of the pictures?" said Cheyenne. She sneezed and blew her nose into a tissue. Cheyenne was allergic to absolutely everything. "Oh god, Wally, I'd hate to think it was because we gave him those pictures. I'd hate to think we caused his death. Do you think we caused his death?"

Wally nodded.

"I'm sure of it," he said. "But then what happened to our pictures? The whole thing sounds so bogus to me. A sudden heart attack, right? The onts must have a mole in the Cincinnati office who killed him. It might even have been that stupid receptionist we just talked to."

"Why do you say that?" Cheyenne asked.

"Did you get a good look at her face?" said Wally. "At her skin? Her skin looked like those rubber masks that Dagmar and Hedy used to wear."

Cheyenne shuddered. Dagmar and Hedy Mandible were the two mysterious ladies who'd taken them out of the Jolly Days Orphanage to their home in spooky Dripping Fang Forest for a trial adoption. After discovering the Mandible sisters weren't ladies but giant ants breeding a race of super-ants to enslave humans and end life on Earth as we know it, the twins managed to escape.

"I hate to say it, but I think you're right," Cheyenne murmured. "I sure hope she doesn't think we suspect her."

"We didn't do anything to make her think we suspect her," said Wally.

"Lucky I still have the negatives," said Cheyenne. "I'll get some more prints made. Who can we take them to, though?"

"Well, we sure can't trust anyone in the Cincinnati office," said Wally. "Let's go to that FBI place in Quantico, Virginia, where they train their agents. Where they have the guys who profile serial killers and stuff. I doubt the onts have planted anybody in Quantico yet."

"How will we get there?" Cheyenne asked. "We don't have money for planes."

"We'll take the train," said Wally. "It's cheaper than flying and a whole lot safer."

The elevator arrived at the main floor. The doors slid open and the twins stopped talking, fearing they might be overheard.

The receptionist switched off the small silver tape recorder on her desk. She hit REWIND and then PLAY. The voices from the elevator were thin and tinny but very clear:

"...to that FBI place in Quantico, Virginia, where they train their agents. Where they have the guys who profile serial killers and stuff. I doubt the onts have planted anybody in Quantico yet."

"How will we get there? We don't have money for planes."

"We'll take the train. It's cheaper than flying and a whole lot safer."

The receptionist hit STOP and slipped the small silver tape recorder into her handbag.

CHAPTER 2

Kill Wally—Also, If It's Not Too Much Trouble, Cheyenne

The figure that reclined on the ninety-foot-long sofa was the size of a humpback whale. The gargantuan Ont Queen was dressed in camouflage fatigues that had been stitched together from twelve military tents. The stub of a large cigar was clamped between her gigantic mandibles.

The queen's couch was in the center of a cavern with an immensely tall domed ceiling. Stalactites hung from the ceiling like fangs from a monster's mouth. Stalagmites the size of oak trees grew out of the floor. A hundred candleholders made of black wrought iron held a thousand lit candles. The walls of the cavern were plated in 24-karat gold. Even the stalagmites and stalactites were plated in 24-karat gold, and they mirrored the flickering candles. There was a strong odor of melting wax.

Hedy Mandible, a six-foot-tall ont wearing a partial mask that covered one side of her disfigured face, switched off the small silver tape recorder the receptionist had given her.

"This is an outrage, Hedy!" cried the queen. "Who are these children and how did they ever get photographs of the buses and the human slaves?"

"My Queen," said Hedy, "the children on the tape are the Shluffmuffin twins, Wally and Cheyenne. I don't know how they got photos of the buses and the human slaves, but I fear Cheyenne might have snapped them after she spoke to the class of mutant children."

"But you told us the Shluffmuffin girl was hypnotized," said the queen. "Isn't that what you told us?"

"I did, My Queen," said Hedy, "but—"

"We are not experts on hypnosis or posthypnotic suggestion," said the queen, "and so we will have to ask your expert opinion. Hedy: Is it customary for hypnotized subjects to go off on their own and take photographs of buses and human slaves?"

"No, My Queen," said Hedy, "it isn't customary, but—"

"Then would it be safe to assume that the Shluffmuffin girl was not actually under post-hypnotic suggestion at all, as we were led to believe?" said the queen.

"Well, My Queen," said Hedy, "I would have to say that, for at least the latter part of her last visit to the cave, it would be safe to assume she was probably in such a light trance that—"

"Was she in a trance or wasn't she?" shouted the queen. The force of her shout blew out a hundred flickering candles. Curlicues of smoke rose from their wicks, giving the room a not unpleasant smoky-waxy aroma.

"N-no, My Queen," said Hedy, "at least not for the last part of her visit, but I'd like to point out that—"

"And would it be safe to assume," the queen

continued, "that the person in charge of this particular posthypnotic suggestion training project was totally and tragically incompetent?"

"Well, My Queen," said Hedy, "I think, in all fairness, that—"

"Totally and tragically incompetent or not?" shouted the queen, blowing out a hundred more candles.

"T-totally and tragically incompetent, My Queen," said Hedy.

The queen nodded her huge head, which made her antennae bob. She removed the cigar stub and opened and closed her giant black mandibles, which looked like huge black sideways pliers and made little clacking sounds as they closed.

"Well, thank you for being so honest, Hedy," said the queen. "I admire a frank admission of sickening ineptitude. I find it refreshing. The Shluffmuffin girl's teaching of mutant children program is hereby canceled. Can you think of any reason why both the Shluffmuffin twins should not now be terminated?"

"No, My Queen, I can't," said Hedy softly.

"Speak up, Hedy!" said the queen. "We can't hear you when you mumble!"

"No, My Queen," said Hedy, louder.

"And can you think of any reason why you should not be decapitated and your body ground up for food?"

Hedy shook her head. "No, My Queen," she answered.

The queen stroked her antennae in thought. "You have been a good and faithful servant, Hedy," she said.

"Thank you, My Queen," said Hedy.

"So we will give you a choice," said the queen. "Would you prefer death by decapitation or death by being dissolved in a vat of sulfuric acid?"

"My Queen," said Hedy, "may I humbly suggest a third alternative?"

"Of course, my dear," said the queen. "Does it include your immediate and painful demise?"

"Not exactly, My Queen," said Hedy. "It involves hiring an assassin to terminate the lives of both Shluffmuffin children."

"Forgive us for having a poor memory," said the queen. "Who was it that hired the Jackal individual to kill Wally Shluffmuffin? We can't seem to recall."

"It was I, My Queen," said Hedy, "but—"

"Ah yes," said the queen, "it *was* you, Hedy. I do remember that. And was he successful? What happened?"

"No, My Queen, he wasn't successful," said Hedy. "He injected Wally with an overdose of insulin that should have given him insulin shock and killed him but didn't. I still don't see how the boy survived."

"What a pity," said the queen. "And did The Jackal try again, dear? What happened?"

"Well, your highness, I believe you know what happened and that you're just toying with me, but I don't mind, I probably deserve it, so I'll play along. The Jackal then tried to kill Wally with a blowgun and a dart tipped with poison made from the poison dart frog, and—"

"And was that successful, dear?" asked the queen. "Refresh an aging monarch's memory."

"No, Your Highness," said Hedy. "As I'm sure Your Highness recalls, The Jackal's aim was off and he missed. And when he put another poison dart in the blowgun, he sneezed and somehow inhaled the dart into his own throat, killing himself instantly."

"Tsk-tsk," said the queen. "One does so hate to lose a professional. A good hit man is hard to find. So what you're telling us, dear, is that, having hired an assassin who was so incompetent he not only failed three times and then killed himself through his own ineptitude, you'd like to try again. Where are you thinking of looking for an assassin this time, a school for clowns?"

"No, Your Highness," said Hedy. "I plan to hold open auditions and choose from among an international selection of the most diabolical professional killers in the world. The Shluffmuffin twins are already dead. They just don't know it."

CHAPTER 3

Somebody Can Always Overhear You

"Who'd like some lovely Roast Beef à la Tarantelle?" asked Shirley, holding up a steaming platter with one of her many arms.

Shirley Spydelle might have been an excellent cook were she a human. But since she was a giant spider, she tended to inject most meat dishes with her saliva and turn them into an easily digestible jelly that most humans didn't seem to appreciate.

"Is Roast Beef à la Tarantelle the one with the green jelly center?" Cheyenne asked.

"Yes, dear," said Shirley. "And I made a really yummy sauce to go with it."

"I think I'll just have the asparagus and the baked potato, then," said Cheyenne.

"Me, too," said Wally.

"Why, what's wrong with you kids?" said Shirley, a mock frown on her face. "Are you going vegetarian on me or what?"

"No," said Cheyenne, "I'm just not too hungry tonight."

"What about you, Edgar?" said Shirley. "Can I sell some to you?"

"You jolly well can, my love," said her human husband, Edgar, in his charming British accent. He had long ago gotten used to spider cooking and had even begun to like it.

Shirley bent to serve Edgar, then turned to Dad. "What about you, Sheldon?" she asked. "Can I sell you some Beef à la Tarantelle?"

"Sure, why not?" said Dad.

Because he was a vampire, Dad wasn't technically alive and no longer had a digestive system. After dinner he would simply cough up his food into the toilet and flush. He was only eating to be polite.

Shirley served Dad and then sat down and served herself.

"Dad," said Wally, "Cheyenne and I have to skip school tomorrow. I hope you don't mind."

"Why do you have to skip school?" asked Dad, chewing his beef.

"We have to go somewhere," said Cheyenne. "Somewhere important."

"Where?" said Dad.

Cheyenne and Wally exchanged looks.

"We'd rather not say," said Wally.

"Why not?"

"Because," said Cheyenne, "you might think it was, well, dangerous or something and try to talk us out of doing it. But we can't be talked out of it, Dad. It's something we have to do."

"Tell me what you want to do," said Dad, swallowing.

"You promise you won't try to talk us out of doing it?" Cheyenne asked.

"I promise."

"Okay," said Cheyenne. "We're going to Quantico, to the FBI thing there, to show them pictures of the buses the onts hijacked with all those people they're holding prisoner in the ont cave."

"Quantico?" said Edgar. "My word!"

"You can't do that," said Dad. "Quantico is in Virginia. That's several states away. I'm not letting any ten-year-old kids of mine go all the way to Virginia."

"I thought you said you wouldn't try to talk us out of doing it," said Wally.

"Well, that was before I found out what you were planning to do," said Dad.

"But Dad, we *have* to go to the FBI," said Cheyenne. "We've got to tell them where those busloads of people are that the onts kidnapped. The FBI has SWAT teams. They could rescue them."

"Why don't you go and see that nice FBI agent you met in the Cincinnati office?" said Shirley. "What's his name again?"

"Cromwell," said Wally.

"That's right," said Shirley, "Agent Cromwell. Why don't you tell Agent Cromwell about this?"

"We *did* tell him," said Cheyenne. "We even gave him some of the pictures. But he's dead now. Wally thinks he knew too much."

"Well, too much or too little," said Wally. "He could have known a great deal, and then again, he could have known hardly anything at all, but he certainly didn't know just enough, because if he had, they'd never have killed him."

"Mmm," said Edgar, mulling this over. "Good point, old boy. They never kill you if you know precisely the right amount, whereas they'll bloody well *murder* you if you know either a goodly quantity or a smidge. It's a matter of degree, you see, a matter of balance. And then, of course, regardless of how *much* of it you know, there's the question of *how* you know what you know, a problem that has made philosophers nauseous since the time of Plato."

That made everybody frown.

"We think somebody killed Agent Cromwell because of the pictures," said Cheyenne.

"And you expect me to now let you take those pictures to Quantico?" asked Dad. "What makes you think that same somebody wouldn't try to kill *you*?"

"Because nobody knows we're going there," said Wally. "We were very careful not to talk about it where anyone could overhear us."

"Somebody can always overhear you," said Dad. "But apart from how dangerous it is, there's the matter of skipping school. Through no fault of your own, you've already missed many days at Dripping Fang Country Day. We just can't afford to give that social worker of yours any reason to send you back to the Jolly Days Orphanage."

"I guess you're right, Dad," said Wally. "All right, we won't go."

Cheyenne looked at Wally.

"What about those poor people that the onts kidnapped on the buses?" asked Cheyenne.

"Maybe there's something *I* can figure out to do about that," said Dad.

"I can't believe you told Dad we're not going to Quantico," said Cheyenne.

They were back in their own room now, with the door closed, switching channels and not finding anything but stupid infomercials and celebrity gossip shows.

"What about all those poor people the onts captured?" asked Cheyenne again. "Are we going to just let the onts kill them?"

"Of course not," said Wally. "We're still going. Right after school tomorrow."

"We are?" said Cheyenne. "You mean you lied to Dad?"

"I hated to do that," said Wally, "but I had no choice. Those people's lives are in our hands, Cheyenne. And probably the lives of all humans on Earth, come to think of it. We'll make it up to Dad somehow."

Cheyenne had a huge sneezing fit and then wiped her nose with a tissue.

"I just wish you didn't have to lie to Dad," said Cheyenne.

"Yeah, me, too," said Wally sadly.

CHAPTER 4

Do Bring Me Some Orphans— But Please, Not Anyone Appealing

"Edgar dear, I've been thinking," said Shirley.

"Uh-oh, always a dangerous activity, that," said Edgar.

They were lying in the living room hammocks after dinner. Edgar was puffing on his pipe and Shirley was spinning silk out of her spinnerets and weaving it into stockings. With eight legs, she was constantly getting runs in her stockings.

"What?" said Shirley, looking up from her spinning and weaving.

"Just kidding, love," said Edgar with a chuckle. "What have you been thinking?"

"Kids," said Shirley with a sigh. "I sure wish we had some of our own. When Cheyenne and Wally said they wanted us to adopt them, it made me the happiest spider on Earth. I felt terrible for their poor father, but so flattered."

"They were fibbing, of course," said Edgar.

"Well, I understand what they were doing," said Shirley. "Trying to save your life, dear. They know that after spiders mate, the lady eats the gentleman. It's nothing personal, it's just what we spiders do."

"I realize that, darling," said Edgar. "Look, we've been through this many times, my dear, but it doesn't make the prospect any more appealing."

"I know, dear," she said. "Why don't we go back to the Jolly Days Orphanage. If we adopted a few of the orphans there, I could have my cake and eat it too, so to speak."

"Or *not* eat it, so to speak," said Edgar. "A smashing idea, my dear, absolutely smashing. When would you like to go?"

"What about tomorrow, right after lunch?" said Shirley. "You know what, though? I don't want to frighten the poor things with the way I look. Why don't you drive over there alone and pick out a few you like? I'll trust your judgment."

"Right you are," said Edgar. "In case you forgot, though, they are rather a sorry lot. Bed wetters, fire starters, that sort of thing."

"Oh, I know," said Shirley. "The poor darlings. Just pick out a few of the neediest ones. Ones that no one else would even consider."

CHAPTER 5

We're Looking for
a Few Bad Men

At the end of the hall on the fourth floor of the musty-smelling office building was a wooden door with a pebbled glass pane in the top half. Taped to the door was a sheet of lined notebook paper on which somebody had printed AUDITIONS HERE. A long line of strange-looking men and women, some of them rather frightening, stood in the hallway.

Inside the tiny office, Hedy Mandible leaned back in her creaky padded chair. "Next!" she called out.

In came a smooth-looking foreign gentleman with a skinny mustache and slicked down hair. He smelled of old sweat and too-sweet after-shave lotion.

"Good afternoon," said Hedy. "Name?"

The foreign gentleman made a deep bow. "Madame, I am Count Fodor," he said with a thick but unidentifiable European accent. "I am de most honored to making your acquaintancesheep."

"Thank you," said Hedy. "Can you tell me a few of your credits?"

"Weeth de greatest of pleasures, madame," said the man. "I heff worked for de finest fomilies een de world. I have worked for de crowned heads of Europe—for royalty, madame. Noturally, I em not at leeberty to say *wheech* crowned heads."

"Naturally," said Hedy. "Would I know any of your recent work?"

"You would know eet een an instant, madame, eef I em able to tell you. Unfortunately, I em not."

"I see. And what sort of methods do you employ?"

The man smiled nostalgically. "Once I pour hemlock eento a patient's ear," he said. "Thees chap was a philosopher. Once I drill a tiny hole een a patient's head weeth a jeweler's drill, so tiny he does not even know. For every patient I make a special prescription, just for heem."

"Thank you, Count Fodor," said Hedy. "Leave me your résumé and your cell phone number, and I'll get back to you. Next!"

Count Fodor bowed again deeply and left. In came a fresh-faced young woman with blond hair, blue eyes, and a wide-eyed grin. She smelled of lavender soap. She was probably in her twenties but looked about twelve.

"Hi there," she said. "I'm Sweetie McMuffin."

"Hi, Sweetie," said Hedy. "Tell me a little about yourself."

"Well, I only do bad people," said Sweetie, "so I love my work."

"Would you have any objection to doing a ten-year-old boy and girl?"

"Oooh, I don't know," said Sweetie. "Would this be a *bad* ten-year-old boy and girl?"

"Pretty bad."

"Well then, it shouldn't be a problem," said Sweetie. "Just out of curiosity, what do they do—not clean up their rooms, not eat their veggies, refuse to do their homework, get sassy with their moms and dads . . . that kind of thing?"

"Worse than that," said Hedy.

"Well then, heck, doing them would be cool."

"Good," said Hedy.

"Leave me your cell phone number and I'll get back to you."

Sweetie waved good-bye and left. In came a husky young man with black hair and a two-day growth of beard. He wore a black pin-striped suit, a black shirt, and a purple tie.

"Hey, howya doin', doll?" said the man in a thick New York accent.

"Fine," said Hedy. "And you are . . . ?"

"Vinnie Colorado," said the man. "I heard ya needed somebody done. Would this be a Mob hit? Because no way am I gonna do any more Mob hits."

"No," said Hedy. "This would be a ten-year-old boy and girl."

"And they wouldn't be connected to the Mob?"

"No," said Hedy.

"Then, hey, no problem," said Vinnie.

"Thank you, Mr. Colorado. We'll call you if we need you. Next!"

The next person was a handsome British

gentleman wearing a suede jacket and a silk
scarf.

"Reginald Webley-Smythe," said the British
gentleman in an upper-class accent. "Formerly
of Scotland Yard and Interpol."

He dropped a business card on Hedy's desk,
sat down, and took out a small pocket mirror to
check his reflection while smoothing back his
hair.

"Thank you, Mr. Webley-Smythe," said Hedy.
"We'll call you. Next!"

The next person was a short man with protruding eyeballs, wild-looking hair, and a double-breasted suit dusted with dandruff flakes and speckled with soup stains. He chuckled to himself continuously.

"Hel-*lo*, missus, heh-heh-heh," he said. "My name is Montag Oppersdorf, heh-heh-heh."

"Thank you, Mr. Oppersdorf," said Hedy. "We'll call you. Next!"

The next person glided in and stood in a dark corner. The collar of his trench coat was pulled up to his nose, and a battered fedora was pulled down over his face. It was impossible to see what he looked like.

"What is your name please?" Hedy asked.

"For now, let's just say my name is Mr. X," said the person.

"I really must have a better name than that," said Hedy.

"That information will be revealed to you on a need-to-know basis," said the person.

"Thank you, Mr. X, we'll call you," said Hedy.

"But you don't know my name or how to reach me," said the person. "How could you possibly call me?"

"That information will be revealed to you on a need-to-know basis," said Hedy. "Next!"

The next person, a young man with a pimply face and hair that looked as though it hadn't been washed in months, entered. He tripped over a samurai sword concealed in his coat and fell. A

machete and two ice picks spilled out of his coat pockets and clattered onto the floor.

"Oops!" said the young man, hastily trying to gather his weapons.

"Next!" said Hedy.

An elderly lady with white hair in a tight bun rolled into the office in an electric wheelchair.

"Next!" said Hedy.

"Now just you hold on one blasted minute there, sister!" snapped the old lady. "How *dare* you decide I'm not suited for the job you're interviewing for without even speaking to me?"

"Well, madam, you're obviously elderly and handicapped," said Hedy. "Those two things right there aren't exactly in your favor."

"Poppycock!" said the old lady. "Granny Cratchitt's my name and offing baddies is my game. Who do you need terminated?"

"What makes you think you're strong enough to kill anybody?" Hedy asked.

Granny Cratchitt reared up and did a wheelie in her power chair. Then she grabbed an ashtray off the desk, tossed it into the air, whipped a throwing knife out of her blouse, and flung it, shattering the ashtray before it hit the floor.

"Any more questions, cookie?" she snapped.

CHAPTER 6

How Perfectly Horrible
to See You Again

 A ll over Ohio, black-hatted onts were drop-
ping mutant children off at orphanages and
leaving mobile adoption vehicles filled with the
distasteful-looking children on downtown city
streets. The onts were counting on tenderhearted
humans, eager to help the unfortunate, to adopt
them. The mutant children would then infiltrate
the humans' families, eliminate their human
brothers and sisters, and begin to destroy human
society from within.

When Hortense Jolly opened the orphanage
door, she cursed herself for not looking through

the peephole first, because she found herself standing face-to-face with Hedy Mandible.

"Well-well-well, Miss *Mandible*," said Hortense, trying to sound as though she were anything but terrified to see her, "what a lovely surprise. Long time no *see*. And how is your lovely sister?"

"Burnt to a crisp, unfortunately," said Hedy.

"Ohhh, yes, I'm so sorry, forgive me," said Hortense, not stepping aside to let Hedy enter. "Yes, I remember now, there was that dreadful fire and your lovely home was destroyed and I did hear that there were, uh, casualties."

"Dagmar was a real roastie-toastie," said Hedy.

"What a terrible experience," said Hortense. "I do hope you've been able to work through your grief. Dagmar was such a wonderful person—kind, sweet tempered, and generous to a fault."

"Truthfully, Dagmar was a horror show," said Hedy. "Demanding, sarcastic, foul tempered, and mean as a snake, though we did somehow manage to get along. But I'm not here to talk about Dagmar. I've come to Jolly Days today to—"

"—to adopt more *orphans*?" squealed Hortense, giddy at the thought she might earn an adoption fee after all.

Hedy shook her head. "No, better than that," she said. "I've brought *you* some orphans to find homes for."

"Oh," said Hortense, her disappointment impossible to conceal. "Well, are they at least exquisite little children with soft golden hair, limpid blue eyes, irresistible dimpled smiles, and impeccable manners?"

Hedy peeked over her shoulder at the mutant children who were waiting just out of Hortense's sight—nasty little Betsy, disgusting little Diane, and repellent little Janet—with their hideous little half-human, half-antlike faces.

"Beauty is, of course, in the eyes of the beholder," said Hedy, "but nobody who sees these children could ever forget them. Would you like to meet them?"

40

"Oh," said Hortense, "are they here?"

"Absolutely," said Hedy.

"I'd love to meet the little dears," said Hortense.

Hedy emitted a shrill sound. Immediately, Betsy, Diane, and Janet loped into view and came hopping up the stairs.

When Hortense caught sight of the mutants, her eyes bugged out of their sockets as if someone were squeezing her neck.

"Hortense, meet Betsy, Diane, and Janet," said Hedy. "Children, this is Miss Jolly. She'll be in charge of you until you're adopted. You are to do whatever she says without question."

"For a human she sure is ugly," said Betsy.

"I wonder how many rats are living in her hair," said Diane.

"Her butt is as big as the Goodyear blimp," said Janet.

A bee flew into Hortense's open mouth, but she was so flabbergasted she didn't even notice.

"As a special advance thank-you for taking such good care of our little darlings," said Hedy, reaching into her purse and withdrawing a sheaf of bills, "I'm giving you a thousand dollars per child now, and a thousand more when each of them is adopted. That's in addition to your usual adoption fees, of course."

Hortense turned to face Hedy. Tears filled her eyes and began to spill down her cheeks, streaking her makeup. She didn't know whether to laugh, cry—or scream.

CHAPTER 7

If You Truly Love Your Work, You Will Probably Make a Killing

"We're sure our ears are failing us in our old age, Hedy," said the queen, "but it sounded just like you said you hired an old lady in a wheelchair to kill the Shluffmuffin twins. Isn't that silly?"

A servant ont held out a golden cup of chilled aphid honeydew, but the queen rudely waved her away. The servant retreated in disgrace.

"I did say that, Your Highness," said Hedy. "But I interviewed at least three dozen assassins, and Granny

43

Cratchitt was the meanest, nastiest, and most diabolical of them all. She had worked undercover for the CIA in Special Ops since the agency was formed in 1947. Her specialty was assassination of foreign espionage agents. She was forced to retire at age seventy, but she fought it in court for two years because she loved her work. She's been freelance since she retired. My Queen, Granny Cratchitt has assassinated more people in more countries than all the Green Berets combined."

"But what can she possibly do from a wheelchair?" asked the queen.

"You should see what she can do with a throwing knife," said Hedy. "You should see what she can do with her cane—which, by the way, has a sword inside and a poisoned tip. Don't worry, My Queen, Granny Cratchitt will rid us of Wally and Cheyenne Shluffmuffin forever."

"She'd better," said the queen. "Because if not, you're going to be taking a pretty long bath. Tell me, would you like bubbles in your sulfuric acid?"

Do You Think I'm a Parrot, Mr. Shluffmuffin?

As the bell rang, the classroom door opened and Wally, sweating and out of breath, tore into the room and scooted to his seat at the back.

The heads of all the kids in class turned to look at him. Some of their heads had furry ears on the top, some had long floppy ears that hung down over their cheeks, and one had eyes on stalks growing out of his forehead. Dripping Fang Country Day was an exclusive private school for the spawn of the sinister folk who inhabited the forest.

"*Pssst,* Cheyenne," whispered Wally to his sister in the seat across the aisle. "I got it!"

"What?" said Cheyenne.

Wally took a folded piece of paper out of his pocket and showed her.

"The Amtrak schedule."

"All right, class," said Mrs. McCaw, their teacher, "we'll start today with history. I assume you all did the reading assignment." Mrs. McCaw had a shrill, screechy voice, and she had a large parrotlike beak where her nose and mouth should have been. "Please take out your history books and turn to page . . . Excuse me, Mr. Shluffmuffin, what have you got there?"

All heads turned around to stare at Wally.

"What?" said Wally.

"I said what have you got there?" said Mrs. McCaw.

"Nothing."

"Come up here and share it with the rest of the class," she said.

Wally didn't move.

"Please bring what you have there up to my desk, Mr. Shluffmuffin," said Mrs. McCaw.

The kids tittered with laughter.

"But I . . ."

"Please bring it up to my desk *at once,* Mr. Shluffmuffin," said Mrs. McCaw.

Wally slipped the Amtrak schedule into his pocket.

"I'm sorry, Mrs. McCaw," he said.

"You have a choice, Mr. Shluffmuffin," said Mrs. McCaw in her shrill voice. "Either bring what you have there up to my desk *immediately,* or else take it in to the headmaster's office."

Wally sighed and brought the train schedule up to Mrs. McCaw's desk. She held out her hand without looking at him. He gave it to her. She peered at the fine print.

"This is a train schedule," she said. "A schedule of trains between . . ." She squinted. ". . . Cincinnati and Alexandria, Virginia."

"Yes, ma'am."

"Why are you reading a schedule of trains between Cincinnati and Alexandria, Virginia, instead of your history book, as I asked you to, Mr. Shluffmuffin?" she asked. "Are you planning a train trip to Alexandria, Virginia?"

"No, ma'am."

47

"No?" said Mrs. McCaw. "Well then, I guess you won't be needing this schedule, will you?"

She tore up the train schedule into increasingly smaller pieces and dropped them into the wastebasket under her desk. The kids laughed openly. Wally tried not to show any emotion at all. It had been pretty difficult to get that train schedule. He'd gotten up at 6:00 A.M., hitched all the way into Cincinnati and all the way back, and now the schedule had been reduced to confetti and was lying in the bottom of Mrs. McCaw's wastebasket.

"Now kindly go back to your seat, Mr. Shluffmuffin, and open your history book as I asked you to," said Mrs. McCaw.

"Yes, ma'am," said Wally. He walked back toward his seat. "Polly want a cracker?" he muttered under his breath.

The kids closest to him broke into peals of laughter.

"What did you say, Mr. Shluffmuffin?" she asked.

"Nothing," said Wally.

"Did you say 'Polly want a cracker?' Mr. Shluffmuffin?"

The kids fell down laughing. They screamed with laughter. They gasped with laughter.

"No, ma'am," said Wally.

"Do you think I'm a parrot, Mr. Shluffmuffin? Is that what you're trying to tell me?"

"No, ma'am," said Wally.

"All right then, Mr. Shluffmuffin," said Mrs. McCaw. "You are excused now to go directly to the headmaster's office and wait for me until the end of class, at which time your father will join us and you can explain to all of us why you think that I'm a parrot."

CHAPTER 9

Naughty Books and Nasty Snakes, a Specialty

Bad Granny Cratchitt rolled her wheelchair down the ramp into the cluttered bookshop and looked around. A sign on the wall read: THE MUSTY BOOK SHOPPE, ESTABLISHED 1905.

"May I help you?" asked a dignified-looking woman with white hair and steel-rimmed glasses on a beaded chain.

"I was told that you had special items for discriminating buyers," said Granny.

"Why yes," said the woman, with a professional smile. "The Musty Book Shoppe carries a complete catalog of antique rare books for naughty children. We have a little-known work of A. A. Milne called *The House at Pooh-Pooh Cor-*

ner. We have another rare Milne work called *In Which Eeyore Makes Everyone Feel So Guilty They Get Diarrhea.* Would you like to see either of those?"

"No, not really," said Granny Cratchitt.

"We also have a rare version of *Goodnight Moon* in which the child bids endless goodnights to his buttocks," said the woman. "We have an even rarer version of *Pat the Bunny* in which the reader is invited to feel such surfaces as bunny poo, boogers, baby throw-up, splinters, and rusty nails."

"Listen, sis," said Granny Cratchitt, "I don't have all day here. I was told you also sell poisonous snakes."

"You've been misinformed," said the woman.

Granny Cratchitt reached into her purse and pulled out several packets of hundred-dollar bills wrapped in thin paper bands and showed them to the woman.

"As a special courtesy to our oldest customers," said the woman, "we do also carry a very discreet selection of poisonous snakes."

"That's more like it," said Granny Cratchitt. "Tell me what you got in stock."

"Well," said the woman, "we have the spitting cobra, which is an extremely aggressive snake. It can spit blinding venom directly into the eyes of its victims and is quite accurate at distances of more than ten feet. It's not an aggressive snake though, and its venom isn't as toxic as that of the king cobra."

"Not aggressive and not as toxic?" said Granny Cratchitt. "Then who needs it? What else you got, sis?"

"We have the black mamba, an African snake whose bite is a hundred percent fatal unless antivenom is readily available and can be given quickly," said the woman. "The black mamba reaches a length of fourteen feet. It flattens its neck to display its hood, it flicks its tongue and hisses loudly, it opens its black cavernous mouth and rears up four or five feet—half its body length—to strike. It's the fastest, longest, and most aggressive of venomous snakes. Two drops of its venom is enough to kill a grown man."

"Perfecto," said Granny Cratchitt. "Put that in my shopping basket. What else you got?"

"We also have the inland taipan, a very rare species from Australia, which is one of the most poisonous of all snakes. It makes the cobra look like a garter snake. One bite delivers enough venom to kill about a hundred people."

"I like that," said Granny Cratchitt.

"Curiously," said the woman, "although it has the most toxic venom of any snake on Earth, the inland taipan is rather shy."

"It's *shy*?" said Granny Cratchitt. "What do I need with shy? Hey, maybe the poor snake is just suffering from low self-esteem. Maybe I should call in a snake psychologist to help it with social situations. *Forget* about it! What else you got?"

"Well, we have the death adder, a relative of the cobra, which has a bite that's lethal in fifty percent of cases in which antivenom treatment isn't available."

"Only fifty percent?" said Granny Cratchitt. "And only when antivenom isn't available?

C'mon, what kind of wussy stuff is that? I do love the name, but the death adder is a wuss. Forget about it. What else you got, sis?"

"Finally, from India we have the king cobra,"

said the woman. "When threatened or on the attack it will hiss loudly, lift a third of its body
length off the ground, and flatten its neck ribs
into a hood. There are two spots, one on each
side of the front of the hood, that look like eyes
and scare most predators away. Its head is as big
as a man's hand, and a grown king cobra can
stand tall enough off the ground to look you
straight in the eye, which makes it a terrifying
sight. A king cobra bite can kill a full-grown ele-
phant in about three hours."

"The king is my kind of guy," said Granny
Cratchitt. "Okay, sweetheart, ring me up for one
king cobra and one black mamba. It's a pleasure
doing business with you."

CHAPTER 10

Mrs. McCaw Happens to Have a Really Gigantic Beak

They had all taken seats in the headmaster's office—Wally, Cheyenne, Dad, Mrs. McCaw, and the headmaster himself, a husky man with bushy eyebrows and a gruff face that was rather ordinary but for the set of magnificent antlers that grew out of his head.

As usual when the headmaster was in the room, Wally and Cheyenne tried not to stare at the antlers, but that was difficult. The headmaster sat behind a large desk made out of rough lumber that had been sanded and smoothed and lacquered to a gloss so high that saliva beaded right up when you spit on it. Not that anyone ever did.

Everybody in the headmaster's office was looking embarrassed and uncomfortable, but Wally was wet with sweat about what he'd done. Not only had he gotten into trouble by muttering something incredibly stupid but he'd also delayed their Quantico trip and lessened the chances that an FBI SWAT team might be able to rescue the captives at the ont cave in time.

Why had he said anything as dumb as "Polly want a cracker?" anyway? And how was he going to get out of this mess? He could always tell the headmaster that Mrs. McCaw had mis-heard him, but then what could he insist he'd actually said? What even *sounded* like "Polly want a cracker?" He ran through the alphabet, trying to think of words that sounded like Polly. *Collie, dolly, folly . . .*

"Wally, do you know why we're all here?" the headmaster finally asked.

"Yes, sir," said Wally quietly.

. . . golly, holly, jolly, molly . . .

"Tell us, please," said the headmaster.

Wally sighed. "We're here to punish me

57

because Mrs. McCaw thinks I said something mean about her."

"That's correct," said the headmaster.

What rhymes with cracker? Backer, hacker, hijacker . . .

"And what do you think she thinks I said?" Wally asked.

"'Polly want a cracker?'" said the headmaster.

. . . lacquer, packer, quacker . . .

"And why would I say something as dumb as that?" Wally asked.

"Because of her big . . ." The headmaster looked at Mrs. McCaw. "Because she happens to have a really huge . . ." The headmaster bit his lip, cleared his throat, and pulled his collar slightly away from his neck. "Because Mrs. McCaw has a rather large beak instead of a nose," he said finally. "A gigantic proboscis that very much resembles the beak of a parrot. That's why."

Mrs. McCaw closed her eyes, dabbed at them with a tissue, and began to sob.

. . . sacker, slacker, smacker . . .

"Sir," said Wally, "I happen to like Mrs. McCaw a lot. I think she's a terrific teacher, okay? In the short time I've been in her class she's already taught me more than I learned in school in the past three years."

. . . stacker, tacker, whacker . . .

"But you haven't *been* to school in the past three years," said the headmaster. "You've been home-schooled at the Jolly Days Orphanage for the past three years."

"That's not the point, sir," said Wally, realizing he'd gambled on the headmaster not remembering his school history and lost. "The point is, sir, that I really respect her as a person. And I think she's a really cool-looking lady. And, frankly, I didn't even notice till you said it now that she has a beak instead of a nose." He looked hard at Mrs. McCaw. "But now that I'm looking at it, I'd say Mrs. McCaw's beak is one of the coolest, best-looking beaks I've ever seen. If *I* had a beak, I'd want it to look exactly like Mrs. McCaw's."

Mrs. McCaw was looking at Wally with something between gratitude and love.

Wally decided to push it a little. "Frankly, sir," he said, "I'm surprised you'd even be talking about the things that make each of us here at Dripping Fang Country Day so special."

The headmaster was losing ground fast and he knew it. "Laudable sentiments, my son, laudable sentiments," he said. "But, feeling as you do, I'm even more unclear why you'd say anything as insensitive as 'Polly want a cracker?'"

"But that's not what I said, sir," Wally answered, still not sure if he was going to be able to pull this one off.

"Then what was it you said?" asked the headmaster.

"Sir," said Wally, an idea taking shape in his mind, "Mrs. McCaw gave us a homework assignment last night, and both my sister, Cheyenne, and I spent lots of time on it . . . but when I saw that one of the boys hadn't done his, I said to my sister very quietly, '*Golly* . . . what a *slacker*.'"

Wally turned to his sister, who was staring at him with undisguised admiration. "Is that what you heard me say, Cheyenne?" he asked.

"Absolutely," said Cheyenne. "'Golly, what a slacker.' That's exactly what he said to me."

Wally turned back to the headmaster.

"It must have sounded to Mrs. McCaw like 'Polly want a cracker?,' sir," said Wally. "Frankly, I don't blame Mrs. McCaw at all. Anyone could have made a mistake like that. Even me."

For a moment nobody said anything. The headmaster, Mrs. McCaw, Dad—even Wally and Cheyenne—shifted their feet, blew their noses, and adjusted their clothing.

"Well," said the headmaster at last, "young man, it appears that there has been a great misunderstanding here."

"Yes, sir," said Wally.

"I'm afraid we've all misjudged you, my boy," said the headmaster.

"Well, thank you, sir," said Wally. "I accept your apology."

"I hadn't offered one," said the headmaster, "but perhaps I should. I'm sorry, son. You deserved better."

"Thank you, sir," said Wally.

Everybody stood up to leave. The headmaster shook Wally's hand very vigorously, getting some real up-and-down motion into it.

Mrs. McCaw came over to Wally and threw her arms around him, crushing her beak into his cheek and causing a sharp pain, which he wisely decided to ignore. Being hugged by a teacher with a beak who had torn up his train schedule wasn't as bad as he'd thought it might be.

"That was the most outrageous snow job I have ever heard in my entire life," said Dad, once they got outside. He gave Wally a huge hug and clapped him on the back several times.

"'Golly, what a slacker?'" said Cheyenne. She laughed so hard she almost peed in her pants.

"I was really sweating there till I came up with the right rhyme," said Wally.

"Well, you did a great job," said Dad. "Now let's head back home."

Wally and Cheyenne exchanged looks. Wally shrugged and nodded.

"Dad, we have something to tell you," said Cheyenne.

"What is it, hon?"

"Well, we're not going home with you now," said Cheyenne.

"Really?" said Dad. "Where are you going, to a friend's house to play?"

"No, Dad," said Cheyenne, "we're hitching a ride into Cincinnati and then we're taking the next train to Quantico."

"I thought we agreed that was too dangerous," said Dad.

"*You* said it was too dangerous," said Wally. "We didn't agree. Dad, we've got to do this. We've got to save those people the onts are holding prisoner in the ont cave."

"Tell you what," said Dad. "Let's all go home now and talk it over. If I can't talk you out of it tonight, I will personally drive you to the train tomorrow, pay for the tickets, and go with you. A little help from the undead might just come in handy."

"Okay, Dad," said Wally. "I'm cool with that."

"Okay," said Cheyenne. "Me, too."

CHAPTER 11

A Glorious Dream Come True

"Why, Professor Spydelle," said Hortense, opening the door wide enough for him to enter, her face and voice lighting up like the Rockefeller Center Christmas tree. "How perfectly marvelous to see you. How's your lovely eight-legged wife?"

"Very well, thanks, Miss Jolly," said Edgar, puffing seriously on his pipe. "It's at Shirley's suggestion that I'm here now, actually."

"Really?" said Hortense, not daring to hope. "And what was her suggestion?"

Edgar entered the orphanage, and Hortense closed and double-locked the door behind him so he couldn't get away.

"As you might recall," said Edgar, "some time ago we were considering adopting a few of your orphans, but with one thing or another, we decided not to. Bad timing or some such. At any rate, Shirley is again rather keen on getting some, so here I am."

"And," said Hortense, her heart beginning to race, "when you say *some,* I gather that you're thinking of ... more than *one* of the little darlings?"

"Quite," said Edgar.

"How ... many of the little darlings were you and Shirley thinking of adopting?" Hortense asked.

"Oh, good heavens," said Edgar, "I should think at least three or four."

Three or four! Oh, happy day!

"Really," said Hortense in what she hoped was a normal-sounding voice, but finding it difficult to breathe. "Three or four. How lovely. Tell me, Professor, was there anything in particular you were looking for?"

"Well," said Edgar, "we were hoping to adopt

66

some children who are particularly needy. Perhaps some who are a bit harder than usual to place?"

Be still, my heart, Hortense advised herself. *This could be some sort of a put-on, some kind of cruel joke. The British often have dark senses of humor, and he could merely be playing with me. But just in case he's serious, I had better go along with it.*

"By a funny coincidence," said Hortense, "we got a new batch of orphans in today who might be just what you're looking for. They are charming but challenging, and—this ought to interest both you and your lovely wife—these children, as I understand it, just happen to be part human and part insect."

"My word!" said Edgar. "Surely you jest, Miss Jolly!"

"No, Professor, I'm quite serious," said Hortense. "Part human and part insect."

"Are they . . . I'm almost afraid to ask this . . . Would the part that is insect possibly be . . . spider?" Edgar asked.

"No, I don't think so," said Hortense. "I

believe the insect part is more ant than anything else. But it's almost the same thing, isn't it—ants and spiders? And it would almost be as if they were your very own natural-born children. Would you like to meet them?"

"Oh, I daresay!" said Edgar.

"Then let me go and get them."

Hortense ran off to get the mutants.

Oh, dear god, thought Edgar, *how could anyone be so fortunate? This is like a glorious dream come true! Wait till Shirley learns about this! She will never again think of having a litter of spiderlings and needing to eat me afterward!*

A moment later Hortense returned, leading the three mutant children. Edgar's jaw dropped and he had to push it back up again with both hands. It had somehow never occurred to him that children who were part insect might look like children who were actually part insect. It was hard to see how he would ever want to cuddle them or tuck them into their little trundle beds or kiss them good night. They would definitely take some getting used to.

"Professor, this is Betsy, Janet, and Diane," said Hortense. "Children, this is Professor Edgar Spydelle."

"Well, he isn't as ugly as *some* of the people who've come here," said Betsy. "The pipe looks pretty stupid, though."

"Professor Spydelle is very interested in adopting a group of you," said Hortense. "And this will interest you—the professor's wife, Shirley, is an insect!"

69

"Get *out* of here!" said Janet. "An insect? What kind—an ant?"

"No," said Hortense, "a spider."

"Yargh!" said Diane. "You married a *spider*? That's sick!"

"We *hate* spiders," said Janet. "They have too many legs. They have too many eyes. Also they look yucky."

"Spiders aren't even insects," said Diane, "they're arachnids."

"Hey, Edgar," said Betsy, "why'd you marry a spider? Wouldn't any human girls go out with you?"

Edgar flinched and fidgeted under the barrage of questions, but he was determined not to be dissuaded. His marital happiness depended on it, if not his very life.

"There'll be time enough to answer all your questions if I decide to go through with the adoption," said Edgar. "But first I've got a few questions of my own. Number one: What makes you so infernally rude? Do you imagine that

70

anyone in his right mind is going to put up with such abominable rudeness?"

"Oooooh, he's a *tough* one," said Betsy. "I *like* tough ones. Hey, Edgar, we're pretty tough, too. You think you could handle us?"

"I could bloody well handle you all right," said Edgar. "The question is whether I'd care to. The question is whether you're even worth the effort."

"How would you handle us, Eddie?" asked Janet. "Would you try to train us like circus animals, with a whip and a chair?"

"If you *acted* like circus animals, I'd bloody well *treat* you like circus animals," said Edgar. "If you acted like children who wished to be members of a loving family, then that is how I'd treat you."

"Oooooh, members of a loving *family*," said Betsy. "What's in it for us to be treated like members of a loving *family*, Eddie-boy?"

"First of all," said Edgar, controlling his temper with difficulty, "my name is neither Eddie

71

nor Eddie-boy. If you wish to have a conversation with me, I suggest you address me by my proper name, which to you is Professor Spydelle. Otherwise, this conversation is concluded."

"Awww, Betsy, now you've gone and made him mad," said Diane. "Did she make you mad, Eddie-boy?"

"This conversation is now concluded," said Edgar. He turned on his heel and strode out of the room.

"You kids are really stupid," said Hortense. "You blew a perfect adoption opportunity."

"This sucks," said Betsy. "I was just sort of starting to like him. Hey, come back! We want to keep talking to you, Professor Spydelle!"

The mutants ran after Edgar and stopped him just as he was unlocking the front door.

"Can we keep talking, Professor Spydelle?" Betsy asked.

"I don't think I care to do that any longer," said Edgar.

"You said we could talk to you if we addressed you by your proper name, which is Professor Spydelle," said Diane. "So we're addressing you by your proper name, Professor Spydelle . . . sir."

Edgar walked out the front door.

"How about if we apologized?" called Betsy. "Would you talk to us if we apologized, Professor? We don't do a whole lot of apologizing, you know. We're sorry, okay? We acted like dorks and we're sorry. Will you please just at least talk to us now?"

Edgar turned to face them. "What's in it for me to talk to three unpleasant children?" he said. "What possible interest could I have in that?"

"What if we *weren't* unpleasant?" asked Janet. "What if we were nice?"

"I honestly wonder if you're capable of that," said Edgar. "Even if you tried."

"Why not find out?" said Betsy. "Why not give us a shot, Professor? If we're nice for long enough, maybe you'd even think about adopting us. If we're not—the first *time* we're not—heck, you can dump us like a steaming load of poop. What do you say?"

Edgar had to laugh at that in spite of himself.

CHAPTER 12

Train Time Is *Your* Time

$\mathbf{B}$ad Granny Cratchitt spread out the Amtrak schedule on her bed. She was wearing a black T-shirt with a white skull and crossbones and the message BAD TO THE BONE.

The Amtrak schedule showed all the stops of the train between Chicago, Illinois, and New York City. After it left Chicago, the train made six stops in Indiana—Dyer, Rensselaer, Lafayette, Crawfordsville, Indianapolis, and Connersville—before hitting Cincinnati, where the Shluffmuffin twins would certainly board. She would have to know ahead of time when they were going to board, and then she would need plenty of time to board herself. It would take her much longer because she was handicapped and would—in addition to managing her personal effects, her walker, and her wheelchair—be carrying two fairly heavy snakes.

Once she was on the right train, she would have seventeen stops from the time it left Cincinnati till it reached Alexandria, Virginia, where the twins would be planning to get off. They'd find out that Alexandria was the closest it would come to Quantico, and that they'd have to take a cab the final twenty-five miles. So after leaving Cincinnati, there were three stops in Kentucky, nine in West Virginia, and five in Virginia. She and her snakes would have nearly seven hours to get the job done.

But how could she know in advance what train the twins would take? And how could she buy herself the time she needed to make it onto the train with all her gear?

———

FAX FROM BAD GRANNY CRATCHITT

TO: Hedy Mandible et al.

SUBJECT: Termination of Shluffmuffin, Cheyenne (a female), and Shluffmuffin, Walter (a male).

MESSAGE: I require at least twenty (20) of your operatives, equipped with cell phones, to IMMEDIATELY take up positions in and around the Cincinnati railroad terminal. THEY WILL CALL ME at my previously communicated contact number AS SOON AS TARGETS HAVE BEEN SPOTTED BOARDING A TRAIN. Operatives will furnish me with TARGETS' TRAIN NUMBER AND TIME OF DEPARTURE from Cincinnati.

I have obtained a schedule of all trains between Cincinnati and Alexandria, Virginia, the targets' presumed destination. I assume targets plan to continue on to the FBI facility at Quantico, Virginia--there is no railroad stop at Quantico. Targets presumably plan to travel the 25 miles from Alexandria to Quantico by cab, a 39-minute ride.

I have already positioned myself in a hotel near a railroad station in a town somewhere between Cincinnati and Alexandria—security considerations forbid disclosing my exact location. I shall board the targets' train when it stops there. OPERATIONS WILL COMMENCE SOON AFTER I BOARD WITH MY EQUIPMENT.

FAX FROM BAD GRANNY CRATCHITT
TO: HEDY MANDIBLE ET AL.
SUBJECT: TERMINATION OF
SHLUFFMUFFIN CHEYENNE (A FEMALE), AND

Everyone Has to Be Happy If These Things Are Going to Work

"Shirley, I'm home!" called Edgar as he opened the front door.

"Did you bring us home some nice orphans?" Shirley called back.

"Come out and see, dear!" said Edgar. He flashed Betsy, Diane, and Janet a warning look.

Shirley ambled into the living room. She was wearing blue silk toreador pants with many legs. The mutants and the giant spider spent a moment in stunned silence, sizing one another up.

"Shirley," said Edgar, "may I present Betsy, Diane, and Janet. Girls, this is Mrs. Spydelle."

"Oh, darling, they look like *lovely* girls," said Shirley. "They *are*, uh, girls?" she added hurriedly.

Edgar nodded, a forced smile glued onto his face.

"She's . . . a lot bigger than I expected," said Betsy.

"Also . . . hairier," mumbled Janet.

"I explained to the girls that this will be a *trial* adoption," said Edgar, glaring in the mutants' direction.

"Yes, of course," said Shirley. "Everyone has to be happy if these things are going to work. Well, girls, who'd like some tea and gingersnaps?"

"We're home!" called Dad as he opened the front door of the Spydelles' house an hour later. He, Wally, and Cheyenne walked into the front hallway. Cheyenne went into the kitchen for a Mallomar and nearly collided with Betsy.

"Betsy?" screamed Cheyenne. "I can't *believe* this! What the heck are *you* doing here?"

"Cheyenne, you old turd!" shouted Betsy. "What are *you* doing here?"

"This is where I live," said Cheyenne. "Wally and I and our dad are living with the Spydelles."

"No way!" said Betsy. "Hey, guess what! The Spydelles are thinking of adopting us. Is that a coincidence or *what*?"

"But how did you even get to meet them?" Cheyenne demanded.

"Well, Hedy dropped us off at an orphanage called Jolly Days, and—"

"You went to the Jolly Days Orphanage?" said Cheyenne. "That's where Wally and I lived for three years!"

"Get *out*!" said Betsy. "Wait, that's right. Hedy said she knew that place because she and her sister, Dagmar, went there a while ago to adopt some orphans."

Cheyenne went to the cupboard and took out a package of Mallomars.

"Betsy, I know what you guys are doing here," said Cheyenne. "I know about the onts' plans to get humans to adopt mutants and have them slowly destroy families from within, like cuckoo birds. You forget I heard Hedy tell you all that in the cave when I was pretending to be in a trance."

Cheyenne took out a Mallomar and ate it, but didn't offer one to the mutant girl.

"That *was* the plan," said Betsy. "We *were* supposed to infiltrate human families and destroy them from within. But you forget that we mutants also want to get rid of the queen. I've got all the mutant kids behind me, Cheyenne. I've got, like, forty mutants behind me. We're going to beat that old bag the queen, I promise you. You even agreed to help us, remember?"

"Yeah, I remember," said Cheyenne. "But you know what? You being here in the Spydelles' home is really giving me the creeps. I know what you think of humans, but I happen to love Edgar and Shirley. I really do love them. They're so good to us, and they're so sweet."

"Hey, chill out," said Betsy. "I admit I didn't think so when I first met him, but old Edgar is cool. He really stands up for what he believes.

And Shirley is a gas. We would never do any-thing to hurt either one of them, I promise you."

"Honest?" said Cheyenne. "You swear?"

"I swear," said Betsy.

"Well," said Cheyenne, "then okay . . . I guess."

"Cheyenne," said Wally, "do you really think it makes sense to help the mutants just because they're less worse than the onts?"

"Sure," said Cheyenne. "Why not? I mean, we all hate the Ont Queen, right? We all want to put her out of business, right? So why not work together?"

They had gone into their room and shut the door to talk without being overheard by the mutants.

"Look, Cheyenne, America is always doing that kind of stuff," said Wally. "And it's always a disaster. We help rebels in one country, even though they're creepy, because we both hate an-other country. We give the rebels all kinds of help, all kinds of weapons and stuff. Then the rebels end up being our new enemy, and they use the weapons we gave them against us. It always happens. It's always a disaster."

"Well, that won't happen with Betsy," said Cheyenne.

"No?" said Wally. "Why not?"

"Because," said Cheyenne, "Betsy's not some rebel country, Wally, she's a half-human *ont.*"

"I still don't think you should help her overthrow the queen," said Wally.

"Why not?"

"Why not?" said Wally. "I'll tell you why not. Because she's a half-human *ont* for one thing, and for another thing, she's a *kid,* Cheyenne. How the heck is a kid like Betsy ever going to be able to overthrow the Ont Queen and her whole entire army of onts?"

"Betsy's not *alone,*" said Cheyenne. "She's got, like, forty or fifty mutants behind her."

"Forty or fifty half-human, half-ont *kids,* Cheyenne. We don't need someone like that helping us. We need someone like the FBI with SWAT teams helping us. That's why we're going to Quantico, okay?"

Dad let himself into the twins' bedroom.

"Am I interrupting a private discussion?" he asked.

"No," said Wally. "Dad, are those mutant freaks really going to be living here? Because if they are, then I'm *not*."

"I find them pretty rude myself," said Dad, "but it's not our house, it's the Spydelles'. If they want to adopt the girls, then that's what they're going to do."

"Well, I refuse to live with them," said Wally. "They're *onts,* Dad. They're the enemy."

"But, Wally," said Cheyenne, "I just got done explaining that we're on the same side."

"Dad, you're not going to make us live with those freaks, are you?" Wally asked.

"I don't think we have much choice, son," said Dad. "Until I can earn some real money, we just can't afford to move anywhere else right now. Unless you want to move back into the Jolly Days Orphanage—which means we'd no longer be able to live as a family—I think this is pretty much what we have to put up with for now."

Wally shuddered and then sighed. "I guess you're right," he said. "I guess we'll have to see if the Spydelles are really serious about adopting those freaks."

"Good," said Dad. "This seems like a good time to discuss this Quantico business."

"Dad, we *have* to go to Quantico," said Cheyenne. "If we don't convince the FBI to send a SWAT team to the ont cave, those poor people the onts captured will die."

"But what if you can't convince the FBI to send in a SWAT team?" said Dad. "What will you do then?"

"I don't know, Dad," said Cheyenne. "Then we might have to try and rescue them ourselves—like when you, Wally, Edgar, Shirley, Hortense, and the orphans rescued *me* from the Mandible sisters."

"There were only two of the Mandible sisters," said Dad. "According to you, there are hundreds of onts in that cave, and they're armed with military weapons."

"That's why we have to try the FBI at Quantico first," said Wally.

"All right then," said Dad. "But you are definitely not going there alone. I am definitely coming with you. Maybe they'll take you more seriously if you're with an adult."

"Okay, Dad," said Wally. "But could you at least try to hide the fangs and wings? I don't think they're going to take vampires any more seriously than kids."

CHAPTER 14

If You've Enjoyed Your Stay, Please Don't Kill the Staff

Granny Cratchitt crouched, motionless, beside the bed in the small hotel room in Ashland, Kentucky.

Whiskers twitching, a scruffy gray rat crept cautiously out of the closet and headed toward a small piece of mozzarella cheese that lay just under the bed a few feet from the crouching old woman. As the rat took its first tentative nibble of the cheese, Granny Cratchitt pounced. She grabbed the rat faster than a cat.

She carried the squirming rodent by the tail into the bathroom, opened the lid of the wicker laundry hamper, and tossed the rat in. There was a brief thrashing about inside the wicker hamper, and then all was still.

There was a knock at the room's only door.

"Yes?" said Granny Cratchitt. "Who is it?"

There was no answer, but a moment later she heard the sound of a key being slipped into the lock. Granny grabbed her cane and, in one fluid motion, hip-hopped to a spot just behind the door as it swung open.

"Oh!" cried the intruder as a strong arm grabbed her from behind and a cold blade was placed against her neck.

"Who are you and what do you want?" snapped a hoarse voice behind her. "You have five seconds to answer before I slice your throat."

"Don't slice!" cried the intruder. "Please, missus! I am only de night maid. I come to turn down your bed and put de chocolates on your pillow!"

"Who sent you?" snarled Granny Cratchitt.

"De hotel monoger!" said the night maid.

"Show me the chocolates."

The maid held out an open hand. Three chocolates wrapped in gold foil quivered in the moist palm of her hand.

"Eat one to prove they're not poison," said Granny Cratchitt.

"But I am on a diet, missus," said the maid. "Eef I eating chocolate, I blow up like a balloon."

"Five seconds to eat a chocolate or you'll bleed out like a hemophiliac."

"I eat, I eat!" cried the maid. "Please, missus, no bleeding!"

The maid unwrapped the gold foil from a chocolate and, with a trembling hand, lifted it to her lips and popped it in her mouth.

"Ugh," said the maid. "Deelicious! See, missus? No poison. But feefteen grams of fat."

"Okay," said Granny. She withdrew the blade and the arm. "Sorry if I scared you, sis. I just can't be too careful in my line of work."

"What ees your line of work, missus?" asked the maid, trying to compose herself.

"I work for the government in Washington," said Granny.

"Oh, den I onderstand why people don't like you," said the maid.

"I can't believe you're actually letting us cut classes today," said Wally.

"It's so cool of you," said Cheyenne.

"Well," said Dad, "it's a really long trip each way, plus whatever time we spend at Quantico. You'd either have to miss a day on the way there or on the way back."

Dad pulled the Spydelles' Land Rover into the lot outside the railroad station and parked. Cheyenne and Wally took their canvas backpacks and got out. Then they and Dad went through the heavy doors and into the terminal.

A tall woman wearing the dark blue uniform of an Amtrak sanitation worker and dark sunglasses followed them into the terminal behind a push-broom with a long wooden handle.

Dad, Cheyenne, and Wally went to a ticket counter.

"Yes?" said the man behind the counter, a chubby fellow with a ruddy complexion and a walrus mustache.

"One adult and two children, round trip to Alexandria, Virginia," said Dad.

"Very good, sir," said the man with the walrus mustache. He punched numbers into a machine and it spit out three tickets.

The female sanitation worker consulted an overhead board that listed all arrivals and departures from the Cincinnati station, then snapped open a folding cell phone and dialed a number. After three rings, the call was answered.

"Yes?" said the voice on the other end of the line.

"Train number one-ninety-five," said the female sanitation worker into the phone in a barely audible voice. "It departs Cincinnati at nine-seventeen. Do you copy?"

"Affirmative," said the voice on the other end of the line.

The female sanitation worker flipped her phone closed and left the terminal, still pushing her broom.

Moving in a well-planned but unhurried manner, Bad Granny Cratchitt dropped a few personal items—toothbrush, toothpaste, hairbrush, and a tiny Beretta .22-caliber automatic—into her small overnight bag, then rang for the bellman. A moment later there was a knock at the door.

"Who is it?" called Granny.

"Bellman," said a voice.

"Come in," called Granny.

There was the sound of a key in the lock, and the door opened. The bellman entered and looked about confusedly. He had a blond buzz cut and skin pitted like the surface of the moon from acne scars.

"Hello?" said the bellman, not sure who had answered him.

Instantly, he felt a strong arm around his

chest and a cold steel blade pressed against his neck.

"What th—?" said the bellman.

"Who are you and what do you want?" snapped a hoarse voice behind him. "You have five seconds to answer before I slit your throat."

"Ah'm the b-bellman," said the bellman with a soft Kentucky accent. "Didn't y'all c-call for a bellman?"

"Maybe I did and maybe I didn't," said Granny. "Prove to me you're the bellman in five seconds or I'll slice you open like a melon."

"Mah c-cart is just outside the door, ma'am," said the bellman. "Mah hotel ID is in the left inside p-pocket of mah jacket."

Granny glanced out the door and saw the rolling cart. She reached the blade of her knife into the bellman's jacket, slit his pocket, and caught his wallet in her hand. Inside the wallet was a photo ID. The guy in the photo looked a lot like the man she held in her viselike grip.

"Okay," she said. "It seems you're telling the

truth. Sorry about your pocket. I'll add enough to your tip to cover the repair. Now put my bags on your cart, and be extra careful with my golf bag."

The bellman shook his head and loaded his cart. When he got to the golf bag he groaned. "What kind of clubs you got in this here bag, ma'am?" he asked. "They made out of lead?"

"Yes," said Granny, "as a matter of fact they *are*. I had them custom made for me in Europe. Lead clubs are the very latest thing there."

"And it feels almost as if those clubs was alive in there," he added.

"My clubs are very special," said Granny. "They seem to almost have a life of their own."

The bellman loaded the golf bag, the wheelchair, and the rest of Granny's gear into her handicapped-accessible van with the retractable ramp. Then she gave the bellman a roll of bills that seemed to more than satisfy him and roared away from the hotel.

At the Ashland railroad station, Granny parked her van in a handicapped space, got herself out of the driver's seat and into her power chair, and swiftly located a porter. By slipping him a fifty-dollar bill, she was able to get him to position all of her baggage on the correct platform without a single comment about the heaviness of her golf clubs.

When the train pulled into the station forty-five minutes later, the porter even helped her up into the train itself with all her stuff and without complaint.

"All aboard!" called the blue-capped conductor, and then with a heavy creaking and groaning of metal parts, the train moved slowly away from the platform and, picking up speed, out of the station.

"Did you see that?" said Cheyenne. She turned away from the window.

"What?" said Wally, who had been peering at his fellow passengers to see if anybody looked at all suspicious.

"Some nice old handicapped lady in a wheelchair," said Cheyenne. "She just got on our train with a bunch of stuff, including a golf bag. I think it's so great that an elderly person who's physically challenged loves golf so much she still wants to play."

"How do you know what's in that golf bag?" said Wally.

"What else could it be?" asked Cheyenne.

"Anything at all besides golf clubs," said Wally. "Spears. Rifles. Rocket-propelled grenades, for all I know. You always assume the best of everybody."

"And you always assume the worst," said Cheyenne.

"That way I'm never disappointed," said Wally.

CHAPTER 15

Snakes on a Train

The train hurtled across West Virginia, past farmers' fields, through tunnels, along highways. *Clickety-clack, clickety-clack,* went the wheels on the slick steel rails.

Behind her rolling walker, Bad Granny Cratchitt moved slowly through the train from car to car, searching for the Shluffmuffins.

The train swayed and lurched, and as she passed between cars, the smell of old machine oil and the sound of the wheels on the rails brought back to her a happy time when she was just a little girl and she rode chugging steam-driven trains across the continent with her father. Every time the train pulled into a station, her father would lead her off the train, hoist her onto his shoulders, and take her up to the front to look at the engine. Even at rest, the hissing, steaming beast seemed to be alive, and the little girl was terrified of it, but her father was so comforting, so reassuring, that she viewed these visits to the engine as thrilling adventures rather than traumatic experiences.

In the fifth car she spotted them. The boy and girl looked about ten, had red hair and freckles, and seemed almost identical. They were sitting with an adult, a skinny man with shiny black hair that formed a widow's peak on his forehead. Nobody had mentioned an adult. She didn't know if the man was related to them. There did seem to be a strong family resemblance, but it was her understanding the children were orphans. Maybe the man was an uncle. Well, no matter. She'd get rid of him before she began her work.

When the man got up and made his way down the car, Granny followed him.

In the space between two cars she found him

looking out at the rapidly passing landscape. She dropped some small change—three quarters and a couple of dimes—onto the floor.

"Excuse me, sir!" she yelled above the *clickety-clack* of the wheels on the rails, the rattle and clatter of the plates of metal grinding together under her feet. "Excuse me!"

The man turned to look at her.

"I'm sorry. Did you say something?" he shouted.

"I've dropped some coins," she yelled. "Would you mind picking them up for me?"

"What?" he shouted.

She pointed to the floor. "Coins! I've dropped some coins!" she yelled. "Could you help me?"

He grinned. "Oh, of course, of course!" he shouted, bending to pick up the change.

Seems like a nice fellow. Pity to kill him. Oh well . . .

As soon as Dad began picking up the coins, she lurched forward and pushed him off the speeding train.

———

When Bad Granny Cratchitt returned to the twins' car using her walker, she was carrying two things: One was a tiny tape recorder with a powerful speaker. The other was a cylinder that released sprays of sulfur dioxide—a substance that smelled exactly like rotten eggs—in short, powerful bursts triggered by remote control.

Passing by the twins, Granny dropped more coins. As she bent to pick them up, she swiftly planted the tape recorder and the cylinder underneath their seats.

When she got to the end of the car, Granny used the remote to trigger both devices. The speaker emitted the sounds of a whoopee cushion. The cylinder emitted the fragrance of rotting eggs.

"Eeeoow," said Cheyenne. "Wally, did you fart?"

"Not me," said Wally. "I thought it was you."

"Me?" said Cheyenne. "I never fart. You're the only one in our family who farts."

Granny triggered both devices again. Passengers on all sides wrinkled up their noses and shook their heads.

"I can't believe you did it again," said Cheyenne. "How gross are you?"

"He who smelt them dealt them."

Granny triggered the devices a third time.

Indignant passengers got up and walked out, shaking their heads and pinching their noses. In five minutes Granny had cleared the car—the only people who remained seated were Cheyenne and Wally.

Granny left the car. When she returned, she was wheeling her golf bag behind her. She laid the bag down on the floor of the car, unzipped the end, and left again. The first snake, the black mamba, slithered out of the golf bag and went in search of prey.

CHAPTER 16

Passengers Are Advised Not to Detrain Until We Have Arrived at the Station

Dad painfully picked himself up from the embankment where he had landed and rolled when he was pushed off. There were sharp pieces of gravel embedded in the flesh of his hands and knees. The departing train was getting littler and littler in the distance.

Flapping his large leathery wings, Dad ran a few steps, then leaped into the air and soared up after the train. Startled sparrows darted out of his way with annoyed chirps. The cool wind felt good against his face. He hadn't flown in a while because it always gave him sore back muscles the next day, but now he had no choice.

Ahead of him, far below, looking like a miniature HO gauge model railroad, was the train that the old lady in the walker had shoved him off. Who she was or why she had done such a thing was quite beyond him.

He stopped flapping and swooped gracefully down over the last car, then dropped onto the roof. Hanging on tightly to the roof of the swaying and lurching train, he made his way, hand over hand, to the very end. Then he got a good handhold and let himself down onto the platform at the rear of the last car.

A well-dressed man and woman holding flute-shaped plastic glasses filled with pink champagne were so surprised to see somebody with leathery wings plunk down from the roof of the train that they dropped their drinks.

"Good evening," said Dad. "Sorry if I startled you. I think you may have dropped your drinks."

The man and woman seemed frozen with fear. Dad picked up the empty champagne glasses and gently put them back in the man's and woman's hands. Then he let himself through the back door and into the last car of the train.

Dad walked down the aisle of the swaying and lurching car, scanning passengers' faces, looking for the terrible old lady. People stared at his leathery wings, but he made no move to hide them.

He reached the end of the car and slid open the heavy door. The *clickety-clack, clickety-clack* of wheels on rails was much louder here. Dad slid open the heavy door of the next car and let himself inside.

He found no nasty old ladies in the next two cars, but in the space between the cars after that, there she was, leaning against her walker, applying bloodred polish to her fingernails. She seemed amazed to see him.

"You!" she yelled above the racket of the *clickety-clack*s and the groaning of grinding metal. "How did you get back here?"

She tossed the nail polish bottle over her shoulder, whipped a throwing knife out of her blouse, and hurled it savagely at Dad's chest. The blade made a sickening *slupp* sound and went in up to the hilt, but this didn't seem to bother Dad at all.

Astonished, Granny Cratchitt swiftly pulled a steel tube from one leg of her walker, aimed it briefly at Dad's stomach, released a pull-down trigger, and fired. The resulting shotgun blast blew a hole the size of a softball through Dad's gut. Granny could see right through Dad's midsection, but the wound didn't bleed, and this didn't seem to bother him at all, either.

Dad grabbed Granny under both armpits and hoisted her several feet off the pitching floor.

"What *are* you?" she yelled.

"A vampire!" Dad shouted. "What are *you*?"

"A poor defenseless crippled old lady," she yelled. "Put me down, you bully!"

A blue-uniformed conductor with metallic gold braid on his jacket and cap came out of the car ahead and was astounded to see Dad holding a white-haired elderly woman up in the air.

"Help me!" Granny screamed. "Help a poor defenseless crippled old lady!"

"Put that poor defenseless crippled old lady down this instant!" shouted the conductor.

"But, sir, she tried to kill me!" Dad yelled. "She stabbed me in the chest and shot a hole through my guts—look!"

"Did you do that to him, ma'am?" the conductor shouted.

"Of course not!" Granny screamed. "Where would a poor old crippled lady like me get weapons like that?"

"Sir," shouted the conductor in a voice that sounded as though it generally got what it asked for, "I insist that you put that poor defenseless crippled old lady down at once!"

Dad shrugged and put Granny down on the heaving steel floor. She gleefully shoved the conductor off the train.

"So long, sucker!" she shouted after him.

CHAPTER 17

Maybe It's Somebody's Pet

At first neither Wally nor Cheyenne had any idea there might be snakes on the train. Then Cheyenne spotted one under the seat across the aisle from them and screamed.

Wally stared at Cheyenne, alarmed, then looked where she was pointing.

"Oh my god," he said softly.

"What's a *snake* doing on this train for god's sake?" Cheyenne whispered.

"How should *I* know?" Wally whispered back. "Maybe it's somebody's pet and it got out of its cage or something. Maybe it belongs to one of those Animal Planet guys."

The snake's scales were dark gray in color, fading to light gray on its belly, and it looked to be maybe ten feet long. It seemed to be studying Wally and Cheyenne. It had beady black eyes, and its long forked tongue flicked in and out.

"Do you think it's poisonous?" Cheyenne whispered.

"Let me see," said Wally, his heart hammering in his chest, his mind racing to retrieve hundreds of pages of stored encyclopedia files in his brain. "Okay, here's how to tell venomous snakes from nonvenomous ones. Venomous snakes have diamond- or triangle-shaped heads instead of round ones. And their eyes look like cats' eyes instead of round ones."

The snake moved out from under the seat.

"So okay," said Wally, "let's see now. That snake has round eyes and a roundish head, so I think we're okay. No, wait. Sorry. Its eyes look a little pointy in the corners, and its head now looks kind of triangular to me. Yep, I'd say that snake is venomous, Cheyenne."

"Great, Wally," said Cheyenne, beginning to cry. "What are we supposed to do now?"

"Well, snakes bite because they're afraid," said Wally. "If you give a snake a choice between biting or fleeing, it'll flee every single time. What you're supposed to do is stomp around and make a lot of noise. Snakes can't hear, but they can feel the vibrations, and they'll hide or flee as soon as they know a human's around."

Wally got out of his seat, took several steps backward into the aisle, and began jumping and stomping around on the floor. The snake didn't move.

"It doesn't seem to be hiding," said Cheyenne. "*Or* fleeing."

"Yeah, I noticed that," said Wally.

"So now what?"

"Let me think," said Wally.

"Think fast," said Cheyenne. "Because it's heading this way."

CHAPTER 18

Downsizing Granny Cratchitt

Dad was outraged.

"You just sent that poor conductor to certain death!" he shouted above the heavy metal sounds of the rushing train.

Bad Granny Cratchitt put her hands on her hips and sneered. "So what are you going to do about it, bloodsucker? You going to bite me?"

"I may!" Dad shouted.

"Really?" yelled Granny Cratchitt. "If you do, you'll make me immortal, and I'll stalk you till the end of time! You know what I think?"

"What?" Dad shouted.

"I think you don't have the guts to bite me, and you don't have the guts to fight an old

113

crippled lady! I think you're a wussy vampire!
What do *you* think?"

"I think you don't know squat about vampires!" Dad shouted.

And then he lifted Bad Granny Cratchitt and her rolling walker up in the air and hurled them both off the speeding train with tremendous force.

CHAPTER 19

If You Can Do a Simple Two-Step, We Can Teach You to Mamba

"Oh no!" cried Cheyenne. "Wally, look over there!"

Wally looked. A second snake had slid out from under another seat across the aisle. This one was a tannish, brownish color, and it was even longer than the first.

"Is that one poisonous, too?" Cheyenne whispered.

"Let me look," Wally whispered. The skin of his scalp and back prickled with fear, but he tried to focus on the shape of the snakes' heads and eyes. "Okay, the first one over there looks like a black mamba, and the second..." He stopped because he'd just realized that the second snake was a king cobra, and anyone over the age of six knew that a king cobra was one of the deadliest snakes on Earth.

"A black mamba?" Cheyenne repeated. "Is that bad?"

"Um, well, maybe not so bad," Wally lied. "Not as bad as, you know, a king cobra or something," he said truthfully.

"But you said it was poisonous," Cheyenne whispered. "Poisonous is bad, right?"

"Well, yes, sure, kind of," Wally whispered. "But for one thing, Cheyenne, snakes don't *like* to bite, okay? A snake will only bite if it can't hide. A snake will only bite as a warning to leave it alone. Skunks don't like to spray you. And bees don't like to sting you, because if they do it kills them. And another thing is... Let's say it bites? Half the time snakes won't even inject their venom into you when they bite—this is true, so help me god—because they're saving it for when they're hunting small animals for food and they don't want to use it all up on *you,* okay?"

He was babbling now, he knew it, but he was nervous and he couldn't stop.

"So even if one of these snakes *does* bite us, Cheyenne—and I'm not saying it *will,* I'm just saying, you know, *even if*—well then, most bites of even *venomous* snakes *are not at all fatal.*"

"Really?"

"Absolutely," said Wally. "The most that could happen is just a little bit of, uh, you know, difficulty in breathing and, uh, paralysis of the arms and legs and stuff."

"Difficulty in *breathing*?" said Cheyenne. "Paralysis of the arms and *legs*?"

"Just a little. Sometimes. But then it passes, and you can breathe and move your arms and legs and everything else, and you're as healthy as you were before you got bitten. *Healthier,* even, because a little bit of snake venom is actually good for you—did you know that? I forget what it does—makes your immune system work better or something . . . I'm not sure."

117

"I don't believe that at all," said Cheyenne.

"Well, okay," said Wally, "that might not even be true. I might have made that part up, but the rest is absolute truth, I swear to god."

Needles, hundreds of needles, were sticking into Wally's scalp. Rivers of sweat flowed down his scalp and into his eyes, down his back and down his sides from his armpits and down his legs from his crotch—he *hoped* it was only sweat. He knew that if they waited for the snakes to attack, he and Cheyenne were as good as dead. Their only hope was to take the offensive before the snakes struck. Which meant Wally had to do something absolutely dangerous and absolutely insane and do it immediately, right now.

He had seen people like Jeff Corwin on Animal Planet neutralize deadly poisonous snakes by tailing them—picking them up in a bare-handed grip on the tail. But they usually had a long hook or a long forked stick to control the snake's head. *If the hand holding the tail is high enough,* he remembered, *the snake finds it hard to launch an effective strike.*

Of course, guys like Jeff Corwin were a lot taller than Wally. And probably they'd practiced on nonpoisonous snakes a few times before moving up to black mambas and king cobras. Well, too bad. You play the snakes you're dealt.

Wally got up and began walking slowly toward the black mamba.

"Wally, what are you doing?" Cheyenne whispered.

"Something stupid," Wally answered.

The snake hissed loudly, flicking its tongue in and out. Then it flattened its neck ribs to display its hood—a rounded flap of skin and muscle on each side of its head that flared out. Then it opened its black mouth, reared up four feet in the air, and prepared to strike.

Two drops of black mamba venom is enough to kill a man, he remembered from somewhere. *How many drops to kill a ten-year-old boy?*

Wally danced past the reared-up mamba and dove for its tail. He'd almost got a grip on it—it didn't feel slimy, as he'd expected, but very smooth—when the snake struck. Wally saw it coming and dodged, missing the darting head by millimeters.

Wally made another lunge for the tail and had to let go when the snake struck again.

After dodging the third strike—*Three strikes and you're out,* he thought idiotically—Wally managed to simultaneously grab the tail with both

hands and stand up in back of the snake, hoisting the tail, which was surprisingly heavy, at arm's length and at about shoulder height.

Furious, the mamba struck again, but its raised tail threw off its timing and it missed Wally by a wide margin.

"Wally, look out behind you!" Cheyenne screamed.

Still hanging on to the black mamba's tail for dear life, Wally whirled to see the king cobra just behind him, rearing up to the level of Wally's

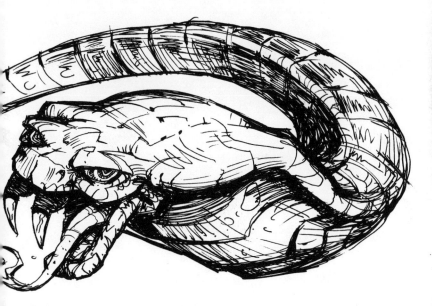

face, not two feet away, hissing loudly, its hood flattened out, eyespots staring at him, its jaws open, its tongue flicking, its fangs glinting.

The king cobra will only attack a human if provoked or in extreme circumstances that threaten its survival, he recalled.

The black mamba struck again, and again Wally, holding its tail aloft, threw off its timing and made it miss. But now Wally, with the tightest possible grip on its tail, pumped his hands rapidly up and down in a crack-the-whip motion and thought he heard something snap.

The mamba thrashed around wildly, and Wally had to let it go, but he could tell he'd done something to it—something serious, maybe even snapped its spine, if it even *had* one.

Now an amazing thing happened. The king cobra shifted its attention from Wally to the wounded mamba.

King cobras feed almost entirely on other snakes, even venomous ones, he recalled from some encyclopedia or other.

Without warning, the king cobra lunged at

the thrashing mamba and sank its fangs into the mamba's neck just below the head. The snakes were in a death struggle and had totally forgotten about the humans.

That's when Dad entered from the rear of the car. In three quick strides he was up to them.

"What in the name of . . . ?" said Dad. "Are you guys okay?"

"Pretty much," said Wally.

The huge snakes were thrashing around, rolling over and over, smashing into the seats. Wally, Cheyenne, and Dad stepped back far enough to be well out of their way.

"Where'd these snakes come from?" Dad asked.

"We don't know," said Cheyenne.

"Why are they fighting each other?"

"Well, I think I probably wounded the black mamba," said Wally. "And then, because it was injured, the cobra attacked it. King cobras feed almost entirely on other snakes, even venomous ones."

"That's a *king cobra*?" shrieked Cheyenne.

"Yeah," said Wally.

"And you knew that and didn't tell me?" said Cheyenne.

"Pretty much," said Wally.

CHAPTER 20

The Truth, the Whole Truth, and a Couple Other Things

"You should have seen Wally," said Cheyenne. "He went over to that black mamba and grabbed it by the tail just like they do on Animal Planet. He was outrageous."

Wally's face was as flushed and red as if he'd been out in the sun all day without sunblock. They were finally off the train. They'd gotten off at Alexandria, and although it had been at least two hours before they were done talking to the police and the animal rescue people, they were done with all of that now and were finally in a cab on the way to Quantico. The cab smelled like somebody had been eating pizza in it, and Wally wished they'd saved some for him.

"You're an incredibly brave boy, son," said Dad. "I'm really proud of you."

"Thanks, Dad."

"How'd you ever have the guts to grab that snake?" Cheyenne asked.

"I don't know," said Wally. "But if I hadn't done something, the mamba would have killed us both. I figured the odds on grabbing its tail were slightly better than doing nothing."

"You thought the black mamba was going to *kill* us?" said Cheyenne.

"Pretty much, yeah."

"I thought you said most bites of even venomous snakes are not at all fatal."

"I never said that."

"You did, too," said Cheyenne.

"Did not."

"Did, too."

"Did not."

"Those were your exact words, Wally—'Most bites of even *venomous* snakes *are not at all fatal.*'"

"All right, I might have said that."

"Why would you say that if it wasn't true?"

"It isn't *un*true," said Wally. "It's *kind* of true. It might be a little exaggerated is all."

"I'm never going to believe you again," said Cheyenne.

"Yes you will," said Wally. "You always do."

"Not anymore," said Cheyenne. "Not ever again."

"Well, kids," said Dad, "we'll be at Quantico in about twenty minutes. I sure hope the *FBI* believes your story about the kidnapped people the onts are holding in that cave."

"Then you'd better let *me* do all the talking," said Cheyenne.

DAN GREENBURG writes the popular Zack Files series for kids and has also written many bestselling books for grown-ups. His seventy books have been translated into twenty languages. To research his writing, Dan has worked with N.Y. firefighters and homicide cops, searched for the Loch Ness monster, flown upside down in an open-cockpit plane, taken part in voodoo ceremonies in Haiti, and disciplined tigers on a Texas ranch. He has not, however, personally encountered any vampires or giant octopuses—at least not yet. Dan lives north of New York with wife Judith, son Zack, and many cats.

SCOTT M. FISCHER glided through high school doing extra-credit art assignments for math teachers, which is kinda boring stuff to draw. Next he went to art school, where he learned to paint even more boring things—like flower vases. However, he swears that since then he has drawn nothing but cool stuff—like oozy, drooling monsters, treacherous villains, and the occasional flower vase ... that has fangs and eats flowers for breakfast!